Skippyjon Jones

JUDY SCHACHNER

• DUTTON CHILDREN'S BOOKS •

AN IMPRINT OF PENGUIN GROUP (USA) INC.

Para mi familia a la A Better Chance House en Swarthmore:
Shayna Israel, Asia Hoe, Patricia Ottley y Julianna Lucre

Especialmente unas gracias a las muchachas hispanas—
Marlene Rijo, Erica Peña y Kathleen Regalado—
por las lecciónes de español para El Skippito

Con mucho cariño,
Mamalita

CIP Data is available.

Published in the United States by Dutton Children's Books,
a division of Penguin Young Readers Group
345 Hudson Street, New York, New York 10014
www.penguin.com

Designed by Heather Wood

Manufactured in China
30
ISBN 978-0-525-47134-9

Every morning, Skippyjon Jones woke up with the birds.

And this did not please his mother at all.
"Get yourself down here right now, Mr. Kitten Britches,"
ordered Mama Junebug Jones.

"No self-respecting cat ever slept with a flock of birds," she scolded. "Or ate worms, or flew, or did his laundry in Mrs. Doohiggy's birdbath."

The lecture went on and on, as usual.
"You've got to do some serious thinking before you leave this room, Mr. Fuzzy Pants," said his mother, "about just what it means to be a

cat...

not a ***bird*** . . .

not a mouse
or a **grouse** . . .

not a moose
or a **goose** . . .

not a **rat**
or a **bat.** . . .

You need to think about just what it means to be a

Siamese cat."

"And stay out of your closet," she added, closing the bedroom door.

But once he was alone, Skippyjon Jones began to

bounce

and

bounce

and

BOUNCE

on his big-boy bed.

"Oh, I'm Skippyjonjones,
And I bounce on my bed,
And once or SIX times,
I land on my head."

On his way down to earth from a gigantic big bounce, Skippyjon Jones shot past his bedroom mirror.

"HOLY GUACAMOLE!" exclaimed Skippyjon Jones.

"What was **that?**"

So up he went again.
And again it appeared.

Then, using his very best Spanish accent, he said, "My ears
are too beeg for my head. My head ees too beeg for my body.
I am not a Siamese cat. . . .

I AM A CHIHUAHUA!"

Back on land, Skippyjon Jones climbed into his toy box and rifled through some of his old junk.

After he put on his mask and sword and climbed onto his mouse, Skippyjon Jones began to sing in a *muy, muy* soft voice:

"My name is Skippito Friskito. (clap-clap)

I fear not a single bandito. (clap-clap)

My manners are mellow,

I'm sweet like the Jell-O,

I get the job done, yes indeed-o." (clap-clap)

Back in the kitchen, Ju-Ju Bee, Jezebel, and Jilly Boo Jones were helping Mama Junebug Jones make lunch.

"Can Skippyjon come out of his room now?" asked Ju-Ju Bee.

"No," answered Mama Junebug Jones. "Mr. Fluffernutter is still thinking."

In fact, Skippyjon wasn't thinking about being a
Siamese cat at all.

With a walk into his closet, his thoughts took him down a lonesome desert road, far, far away in old Mexico. . . .

Not long into his journey, a mysterioso band of Chihuahuas appeared out of the dust.

"¡*Ay, caramba!* Who goes there?" asked Skippyjon Jones.

"We go by the name of Los Chimichangos," growled Don Diego, the biggest of the small ones. "Who are you?"

"I am El Skippito, the great sword fighter," said Skippyjon Jones.

Then the smallest of the small ones spoke up.

"Why the maskito, dude?" asked Poquito Tito.

"I go incognito," said Skippito.

"Do you like rice and beans?" asked Pintolito.

"*Sí*, I love mice and beans," said Skippito.

"He might be the dog of our dreams," whispered Rosalita.

"Perhaps," said Tia Mia. "If he knows the secret password."

Leaning toward Don Diego, El Skippito half sneezed, half spoke the secret password into the Chihuahua's very large ear.

"aaaaAAAAAAAAHHCHOOOO

"Bless you," said Don Diego.
"*Gracias*," said Skippito.

"Then it is true," decreed Don Diego.

-PICHU!"

"*Yip, Yippee, Yippito!*

It's the end of Alfredo Buzzito!

Skippito is here,

We have nothing to fear.

Adiós to the bad Bumblebeeto!"

Then all of the Chimichangos went crazy loco.

First they had a fiesta.

Then they took a siesta.

But after waking up, the Chimichangos got down to serious bees-ness.

Using his paw, Don Diego drew a picture in the sand of the Great Bumblebeeto for Skippito to see. A hush grew over the Chimichangos so great that one could hear a whisker drop.

"Alfredo Buzzito," whispered the crowd. "El Blimpo Bumblebeeto Bandito."

"*Sí*," said Poquito Tito. "The Bandito steals our *frijoles*."

"Not your beans!" cried Skippito, outraged.

"*Sí*," Poquito continued:

"Red beans, black beans,

Boston baked, and blue,

Cocoa, coffee, kidney beans,

Pinto, and jelly too!"

"And now he comes for us," Poquito added.

"*¿Por qué?*" asked Skippito.

"Because we are full of the beans too."

Then Don Diego stood tall and in his most somber voice declared, "*Yo quiero frijoles—*"

"Huh?" asked Skippito.

"The dude just wants his beans back," said Poquito Tito. "And you are the dog for the job."

"Me?" asked Skippito.

Then all of the Chimichangos turned toward Skippito, the great sword fighter.

But poor Skippito had no time for a plan, because in the blink of an eye a gigantic shadow darkened the landscape. The Chimichangos scattered in all directions.

"*Vamos*, Skippito—or it is you the Bandito will eato!" they cried.

Skippito stood his ground, BUT his legs shimmied and shook like the Jell-O, and his teeth chattered like the castanets.

Then in a *muy, muy* soft voice, he said, "My name is Skippito Friskito. I . . . fear . . . not a . . . single bandito."

But Alfredo Buzzito flew straight for Skippito, until the bean-eating Bandito hovered only inches away from the great sword fighter's face.

"HOLY FRIJOLES!" cried Skippito as he thrust his sword in the air.

POP!

Suddenly, **POP!** went the Bandito, landing on Skippito's sword. And quicker than one could say "Chihuahuas, cheese, and crackers," every kind of bean came spilling out of Alfredo Buzzito, the Bumblebeeto Bandito.

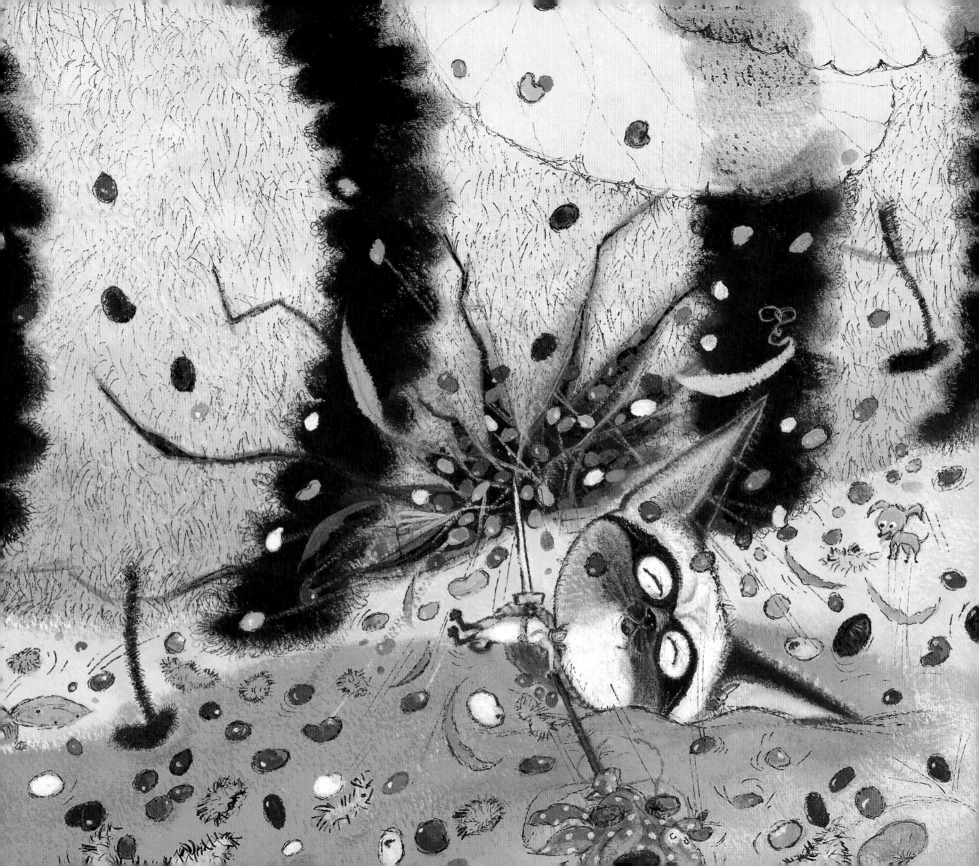

Then all the doggies burst into song:

"Yip, Yippee, Yippito! (clap-clap)

Our hero is El Skippito! (clap-clap)

He's the dog of our dreams

Who delivered the beans,

(clap-clap)

And now we can make our burritos!"

But back at home, there was such a ruckus coming from Skippyjon's room that Mama Junebug Jones and the girls just had to find out what was going on. They raced down the hall to the kitty boy's room . . .

Bangito!

CRASHito!

POP-ito!

Skippito!

just in time to see Skippyjon's closet exploding!

Then out flew candy, beanbag doggies, and the kitty boy with his birthday piñata on his head. "Skippyjon Jones!" everyone cried.

"Hola, muchachitas,"
he said in a *muy, muy* soft voice.

Mama Junebug Jones lifted up Skippyjon and covered his head with furry purry kisses. "What am I going to do with you, Mr. Cocopugs?" she scolded.

That night, when he was supposed to be
going to sleep, Skippyjon began to bounce
and bounce on his big-boy bed.

"Oh, I'm Skippyjonjones,

With a mind of my own,

And I'll bounce on my bed for hours.

I know I'm a cat,

But forget about that . . ."

"Say good night, Skippyjon
Jones," called his mama.
"*Buenas noches, mis amigos*,"
said Skippyjon Jones.